I'M A PIG

By Sarah Weeks ♥ Illustrated by Holly Berry

LAURA GERINGER BOOKS
An Imprint of HarperCollinsPublishers

I'm a pig, I'm a pig,

and I don't give a fig
if you call me a pig,
'cause that's what I am.
I'm a pig, I'm a pig,

and I'm happy as a clam

that I'm not an armadillo

or a lion

or a lamb.

I'm a pig, I'm a pig,
and I'll do a happy jig
if you say, "What a pig!"

For there isn't any doubt—
I'm a pig, I'm a pig
from my tail to my snout,
and acting like a pig
is what it's all about.

I can oink at the moon,

I can wallow in the mud,

I can grin like a goon
as I gobble down a spud.
And I think to be pink
is an honor and a treat.
Besides, it goes so nicely
with my shiny black feet.

I'm a pig, I'm a pig,
and my brain is very big.
Nothing's smarter than a pig.
Look it up—it's true!

I'm a pig, I'm a pig.

I don't blame you if you're blue.

If I were only human,

I'd be disappointed too.

I can just lie around
grunting grunts all day
with my nose to the ground—
not a truffle gets away.

And I feel I could squeal—I'm so happy to be me!

A pig is just the absolutely perfect thing to be.

I'm a pig, I'm a pig,

and I don't give a fig

if you call me a pig,

'cause that's what I am.

I'm a pig, I'm a pig,
and I'm happy as a clam
that I'm not a little puppy
or a guppy or a camel

or a goose

or a moose

or a yellow-bellied mammal—no,

I'm not an armadillo or a lion or a lamb.

I am simply tickled pink

to be exactly what I am.

To Gabe and Natty
—S.W.

To Ellie—
May you always be happy to be just who you are
—H.B.

I'm a Pig   Text copyright © 2005 by Sarah Weeks   Illustrations copyright © 2005 by Holly Berry   Manufactured in China.   All rights reserved.   No part of this book may be used or reproduced in any manner whatsoever without written permission except in the case of brief quotations embodied in critical articles and reviews. For information address HarperCollins Children's Books, a division of HarperCollins Publishers, 1350 Avenue of the Americas, New York, NY 10019.   www.harperchildrens.com Library of Congress Cataloging-in-Publication Data   Weeks, Sarah.   I'm a pig / by Sarah Weeks ; illustrated by Holly Berry.— 1st ed.   p. cm.   Summary: In rhyming text, a happy pig proclaims the joys of her porcine life.   ISBN 0-694-01075-8 — ISBN 0-06-074344-1 (lib. bdg.)   [1. Identity—Fiction. 2. Self-esteem—Fiction. 3. Pigs—Fiction.] I. Berry, Holly, ill.   II. Title.   PZ8.3.W4125Im 2005   [E]—dc22   2004002898   CIP   AC   Typography by Alicia Mikles   1 2 3 4 5 6 7 8 9 10   ❖   First Edition